GET READY...GET SET...READ!

WHAT A DAY FOR FLYING!

by
Foster & Erickson

Illustrations by
Kerri Gifford

BARRON'S

What a day for flying!

Trish was in her dish.
Pat had on her hat.

"Just look," said Trish.

"It is a dream come true."

Swish....
Pat's hat went flying off.

"Oh, no!" said Pat.
"There goes my hat."

Pat's hat went flying...

by Ned and Ted.

"Help," said Pat.
"Please get my hat."

Ned and Ted sped away
to get Pat's hat.

Pat's hat went flying
by the bug club.

It went flying by
slim Jim and the lop.

"Please," said Pat.
"Help get my hat."

Slim Jim, Ned, the lop,
and Ted all sped away
to get Pat's hat.

The fat rat and Ed
saw Pat's hat.

Pat's hat went down
with a plop and came to
a stop on the see-saw.

"Help, help," said Pat.
"Please get that hat."

But swish,
the hat went flying off.

Away they all sped—
slim Jim and Ned,
the lop and Ted,

the fat rat and Ed—
to get Pat's hat.

With a swish and a drop
the hat came to a stop
on top of Pop.

"Up there," said Pat.
"Let's get my hat."

Slim Jim and Ned,
the rat and Ed,
the lop and Ted,

and Trish and Pat
went up, up, up
to get Pat's hat.

"Tug, Pat, tug," they said.
And she did.

The hat went down,
and Pat went down.

They all went down
on top of Pat's hat.

Pat's hat was flat.

What a day for Pat's flying hat!